A DAY IN THE LIFE OF
OSCAR
THE GROUCH

By Linda Hayward
Illustrated by Bill Davis

(A Day in the Life of Oscar the Grouch)

A SESAME STREET/READER'S DIGEST KIDS BOOK

Published by Reader's Digest Young Families, Inc.,
in cooperation with Children's Television Workshop

My name is Oscar the Grouch, and this is the street where I live. I bet you think that being a grouch on Sesame Street is a lot of fun. Well, let me tell you something. A day on Sesame Street is just like any day on any other street.

BUMP! BUMP! BUMP! At six o'clock every morning the newspaper carrier delivers newspapers to the building next to my can. What a terrible noise to wake up to. I love it. It's that BUMP! BUMP! BUMP! that gets me off to a nice grouchy start every morning.

At seven o'clock in the morning I eat breakfast. Today I'm having orange rinds, rotten eggs, burned bacon, and stale bread crumbs. What a great meal! But I'm sure the breakfast at your house is just as good.

Oh, no! Here come my neighbors to get their papers.
"Good morning, Oscar!" says Ernie.
"Good morning, Oscar!" says Grover.
"Good morning, Oscar!" says Prairie Dawn.
AAGGH! Even burned bacon tastes bad after three "Good mornings" in a row.

Eight o'clock in the morning is one of those nice times in the day when a grouch can really relax. Everyone is hurrying to school or to work. Rush, rush, rush! No one has time to stop and say hello.

Isn't it wonderful?

The mail carrier comes at nine o'clock. Today she delivers four letters to the Count. Once again, there is no mail for me. So who wants a silly old letter, anyhow?

Ten o'clock in the morning is cleanup time on
Sesame Street. Big Bird starts sweeping and dusting
and dusting and sweeping.

I can't stand cleanup time. I keep thinking, "There
goes another great collection of trash."

At eleven o'clock in the morning some of
the people around here do chores and errands.

Bert does his laundry
at the Laundromat.

Biff takes his paycheck to the bank.

Rodeo Rosie picks up
her cleaning at the cleaners.

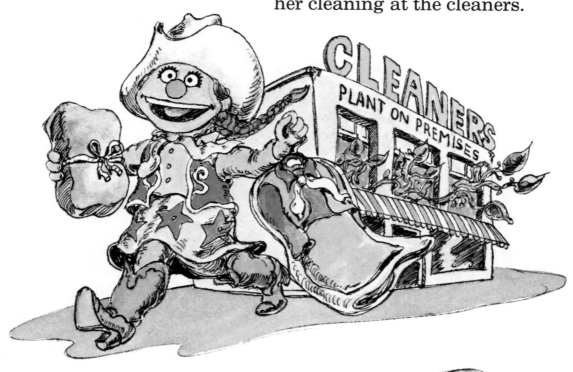

And what about me?
Well, my favorite chore is
waiting for the Mudman's
delivery. Heh-heh-heh.

It's twelve o'clock noon, and that's lunchtime. I don't
know about your neighborhood, but on Sesame Street
friends share their lunches. But grouches don't share.
I would hate to part with any of my delicious peanut
butter and sardine sandwich.

At one o'clock, right after lunch, it's naptime. Even Barkley takes a nap. I just happen to like to play my trombone at one o'clock in the afternoon. Can I help it if Barkley doesn't appreciate great trombone playing?

At two o'clock in the afternoon a lot of people go to the park. There's just one thing I don't understand. The joggers and walkers and bird-watchers and kite flyers like to visit the park on a nice sunny day.

I only go to the park when it rains.

By three o'clock in the afternoon most of the kids are home from school and playing games. They're all doing things they like to do.

Around this time I do something I like to do, too. I complain.

"Hey, Barkley, cut that out! Hey, Prairie Dawn, there's too much shouting! Hey, Ernie, stop laughing!"
We grouches don't like to see anyone having a good time.

At four o'clock on Tuesday the bookmobile comes to
Sesame Street. Well, it is now four o'clock on Tuesday
and that is why I am standing in a line in this crowded
bookmobile. I am waiting to check out my favorite
book—*Mother Grouch Rhymes*.

At last! My favorite time of day! Rush hour!
At five o'clock in the afternoon everyone who has been
somewhere else working all day begins rushing home.
Cars are stuck in traffic. People are tired and hungry.
Motors are rumbling. Tummies are grumbling. Even
cheerful people are a little bit grouchy.

Isn't it wonderful?

At six o'clock in the evening I eat my supper. I suppose you eat your supper in the evening, too.

Tonight I am having pizza. Now I ask you, is there anything more delicious than pizza with banana slices on top?

At seven o'clock in the evening Ernie takes his bath.

Here at Oscar's can it's also bathtime, but not for me.
Slimey, my pet worm, takes his bath at seven o'clock, too.
Of course, he takes a mud bath. Heh-heh-heh.

At eight o'clock it's storytime. Over at Big Bird's nest
Big Bird reads to all the little birds. They just love a good
book. Personally, I can't stand happy endings.

Whew! Now it's bedtime—nine o'clock. Everybody turns out the lights. Everybody snuggles into bed. At last—peace and quiet.

Now it is time for me to practice my trombone again.

What a perfect ending to another yucchy day on Sesame Street.